Uncle Albert's Flying Birthday

Sarah Wilson

SIMON AND SCHUSTER BOOKS FOR YOUNG READERS
Published by Simon & Schuster Inc.
New York · London · Toronto · Sydney · Tokyo · Singapore

A Note From The Baker~
Soap that's baked in
real~life
cakes
will give
everybody
Stomachaches!
Love,
    the Baker

SIMON AND SCHUSTER BOOKS FOR YOUNG READERS
Simon & Schuster Building, Rockefeller Center,
1230 Avenue of the Americas, New York, New York 10020.

The text for this book is set in 18 pt. Horley Old Style.
The display type is Goudy Cursive.
The illustrations were done in watercolor and pencil.

Designed by Vicki Kalajian

Manufactured in Hong Kong

10 9 8 7 6 5 4 3 2 1

Library of Congress Cataloging-in-Publication Data
Wilson, Sarah. Uncle Albert's flying birthday.
Summary: Jennifer Justine and her brother William
must take their baths after all when
a sleepy baker puts soap powder instead of
flour in Uncle Albert's birthday cake.
[1. Baths—Fiction. 2. Birthdays—Fiction.]
I. Title. PZ7.W6986Un 1991 [E]—dc20 90-36158

ISBN 0-671-72793-1

For my editor, Pam Pollack,
chef's choice —SW

Jennifer Justine would not take a bath.
Neither would her brother, William.
"We take baths every day," Jennifer Justine
complained. "We want a day off."

Everyone agreed that Jennifer Justine and William could have the day off. After all, they'd been taking baths for years; and even though they would celebrate Uncle Albert's birthday in the park this particular day, the family decided just to *pretend* that Jennifer Justine and William were clean—not that it would be easy (which, of course, it wasn't).

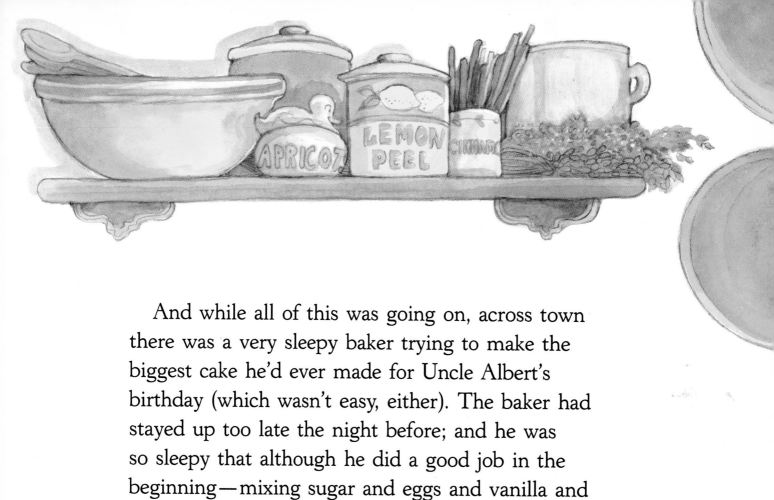

And while all of this was going on, across town
there was a very sleepy baker trying to make the
biggest cake he'd ever made for Uncle Albert's
birthday (which wasn't easy, either). The baker had
stayed up too late the night before; and he was
so sleepy that although he did a good job in the
beginning—mixing sugar and eggs and vanilla and
spices—he didn't do very well in the end—reaching
for a bag of soap powder instead of flour!

The soap powder baked as well as flour and the cake
turned out splendidly, so the baker decorated it and
delivered it to the park for Uncle Albert.

Jennifer Justine and William's parents cheered
when they saw the cake.

Aunt Rowena piled it high with candles, Uncle Albert blew them out, and then everyone sat down to eat, including Jennifer Justine and William, who were not as scrubbed and squeaky-shiny as the rest of their family, although they pretended not to notice.

"A *most* unusual flavor!" Aunt Ella exclaimed.
"The most original I've ever tasted!" said
Uncle Dobbs.
"Wonderful!" shouted Aunt Rowena.
"A masterpiece!" sighed Uncle Albert.

Everybody agreed—everybody, that is,
except Jennifer Justine, who made a face.
"It tastes like *soap*!" she said.
"BUBBLE soap!" added William.

But no one was listening to the two children, whose complaints were all at knee-level; and they were swept along politely with the others to drink Aunt Ella's lemonade—glasses and pitchers and pails of nice, icy, lemony lemonade.

And not long after that, having eaten so much
cake and having gulped down so much lemonade,
one by one by one...

they began to rise up into the air, all of them!
Heels and bows and starched shirts and sashes!

No one minded, of course. It was the kind of magic
that everyone hopes will happen at a birthday party
and seldom does, but still, it was a surprise.

Aunt Ella popped up first, and seemed to like it.

"A great view from up here, Dobbs!" she called out.

"I *knew* that cake was full of soap!" said Jennifer Justine as she lifted off the ground.

"BUBBLE soap!" said William, flying up behind her.

And like big balloons in birthday clothes, the picnic party drifted up through the trees and went bobbing gently along a riverbank.

Below them two big dogs had wandered over to Uncle Albert's birthday table and were helping themselves to leftover slices of his cake—washing it down, of course, with what was left of Aunt Ella's lemonade.

It wasn't long before they,
too, were up in the air,
as well as three ducks,
two raccoons, four squirrels,
and a baby mouse—

all floating just as peacefully up through the
trees and along the riverbank, following behind
Jennifer Justine and William, barking and quacking
and squeaking contentedly, until…

one after the other after the other
they came down to earth in
Mr. Doobey's duck pond,
turning it into the soapiest,
sudsiest, bubbliest bath water
that anyone had ever seen

(from the cake crumbs *everywhere* on Jennifer Justine
and William, all of which, turned instantly into soap)!
Everyone had a wonderful time.

"I've never flown before," murmured Aunt Rowena
contentedly.

"What a lovely day for it," said Uncle Albert,
"and for swimming, too! This has been the most
entertaining afternoon of my life!"

"We should find the baker and ask him for the recipe!" said Aunt Ella.

"Let's go now!" agreed Aunt Rowena, so out they all climbed, soapy and satisfied, and trailed off and over a hill toward town, leaving a slick, sudsy trail and also, for just that moment, completely forgetting about Jennifer Justine and William...

who with the dogs and ducks and raccoons and squirrels and baby mouse, splashed their own way to the dry grass and sat thinking about it all.

"We've had a good time," said William, "but I *knew* they'd find some way to make us take a bath!"

"They always do," said Jennifer Justine, blowing bubbles off her fingers.

But you could tell by looking at her
that she didn't mind a bit — not for
a minute — and neither did William.